PUGAVENTURE
How the Pug Got Its Short Tail

Written by Joanah Adewale

Illustrated by Bryony Dick

Conscious Dreams
PUBLISHING

Pugaventure: How the Pug Got Its Short Tail

First Printed in United Kingdom 2022

Published by Conscious Dreams Publishing

Edited by Elise Abram and Daniella Blechner

Illustrated and typeset by Bryony Dick

www.consciousdreamspublishing.com

@consciousdreamspublishing

ISBN: 978-1-913674-99-1

Dedication

To my family for encouraging me to live my life
to the fullest.

Chapter 1
THE BONGOE DANCE

At the beginning of the yackety-yack years (when the world was so new and all), spring had just met summer, and summer had just met spring, and in the ancient African desert lived a land called the Pugs' Premises. This land was not very far from Loving Labrador Land, which was full of puppy love. In that very limited land lived a go-getting grumble of pugs with a great, infinite source of playfulness and gratefulness.

In this mystical land were three playful pugs that had three interesting names: Clowdie, Cuddles, and Coco. These pugs were not like any pugs — they were like the Three Musketeers, especially since they were triplets. Well, these pugsketeers were different because they had one slight problem: they were cowards when it came to one particular pug (**KEEP THIS PUG IN MIND**). These pugs weren't really the pugs we see today— these pugs were very different. Their tails were probably as long as a tree branch. Well, it can be quite easy to get one that long, especially if you lie a lot.

When it was a hot, sunny day, most of these pugs would play Purky Pugball (which is a pug version of football, but you move the ball with your muzzle) whilst some of the older pugs were sunbathing or having a cool swim in the Humbaba river.

One fateful day, the pugs pathered not at all far from the Bongojo tree and bongoed under the shimmering sun. The three pugsketeers (like I said) were very clever. If they didn't want to do something, it would be quite hard for anyone to make them do it, especially when it was Bongoe Day. It was really quite boring because what all the little pugs had to do was to watch their parents do a dance. It was a very silly dance, quite embarrassing, actually, since the dance went a bit like this: shake your bottom and twirl around (if you can) as you dance with your partner (if you have one), and for the Big Finale, you **KISS! YUCK!** It was torture for the eyes to see because they would do it over and over again until it was sunset.

The little pugs would sneak out when the adult pugs turned around to kiss and then go to their treehouse when they were bored (as I said, they were clever). Once it was all finished, they would come back, pretending to look exhausted and telling their parents they were practising the traditional bongoe dance, except their tails would grow since they had lied.

2

Chapter 2
THE TRIPLETS QUARREL

Now, my friends, remember when I told you I was going to introduce you to a certain type of pug? Well, now I can tell you about that mysterious and yet to be known character. This mysterious character is called Presumptuous Pugie. Yes, he is known as Presumptuous Pugie because—guess what? He is presumptuous. He is very nastignorrant to all of pugkind. He is the most nastignorrant of the nastignorrants. He will not listen to anybody, including himself. Yes, that's right—not even to himself.

This pug was very mean and cheeky. He took the three pugsketeers' ball whilst they were not looking and hid it in his pug playhouse. Remember when I told you at the very start about how it can be very easy for a pug's tail to grow as long as a tree branch if they lied a lot? Well, friends, Pugie is that pug.

The three pugsketeers were very smart. They knew that if they turned their backs on Pugie, something bad would happen. They were pugsolutely right, because when they looked back to see if Pugie had done something, they saw that their ball was gone.

'Oh, come on. I told you, Clowdie: if you didn't look after our ball whilst we were trying to get our kite from the tree,

3

Pugie would take it!' said Cuddles, very angrily.

'It's not my fault because you know I get distracted very easily! By the way, you know that I'm the favourite child, and I could tell Mummy you wore her makeup to a pug party, so you'd better be nice,' Clowdie replied.

'**UGH!** You are so annoying! Why can't you just mind your puggy business sometimes? Everything is always about you, isn't it?' said Cuddles.

'I'm sorry, but I thought I said you should be nice—isn't that right, Coco?'

Now, these pugsketeers didn't always get along, and every time the argument was on pause, the two pugs (Cuddles and Clowdie) always asked Coco whose side she was on. That mostly left her in an intense spot because she'd always been stuck in the middle of these two pugs, and she was sick of them arguing and third-wheeling her.

She replied, 'Enough of this...both of you! Both of you are selfish because you never think about me. You always make me choose between you two, and it annoys me so much. For goodness' sake! Also, you sometimes third-wheel me, and I feel left out. Finally, you asked me the silliest question of all time: who do I love the most? My answer is that **I LOVE YOU BOTH!**'

Did I mention that Coco could be a very shy pug, and she needed to find someone to boost her confidence? Well, if I didn't, there's that piece of information.

The two other pugs were so shocked because Coco had never stood up to them like that before, and they stood there like statues.

There was a long, awkward silence, and no one dared speak until Cuddles finally broke it. 'W-wow, Coco, I didn't know you felt that way, especially when we argue. I guess we have been selfish, and we never thought about you.'

Clowdie suddenly interrupted her. 'Speak for yourself. We all know you always start the arguments, and it's also not my fault you feel that way, Coco, because you never join in the games when we want you to.'

Coco's face turned red with embarrassment, and she knew straight away that she shouldn't have started the conversation. Plus, it wasn't her fault that she was a shy pug, and Clowdie should have respected that and not mentioned it, especially since Coco was her sister.

Cuddles glared at Clowdie with bloodshot eyes and said, 'First of all, don't talk to Coco like that! Second of all, **I DO NOT** start all of our arguments—isn't that right, Coco?'

Coco was fuming. 'This is exactly what I'm talking about!'

Cuddles and Clowdie looked at each other with guilt in their eyes. They both apologised and tried to include Coco in more things from then on.

Chapter 3
FACING PUGIE

Now, I'm sure you remember me saying something about the pugsketeers being really scared of Pugie. Well, because of that, they thought of a silly idea to waste their time asking all the other pugs about the missing ball instead of getting to the point by going to Pugie first. However, now it was time to face their fear of going to Pugie. Face to face. Not to mention that these pugs were not only going to ask if he had the ball (which they knew he had), but they were going to have to hold their breath while talking to him. This was because his breath stank. Yes, my readers—his breath was stinky. Never, ever had he brushed his teeth unless it was a special occasion, so they had to suffer just to talk to him. The trio walked to his messed-up playhouse—or should I say his dump den—whilst their legs were wibbling and wobbling. They checked to see if anyone was there.

'Is...anyone...h-h-here,' stammered Clowdie.

'So much for brave pugsketeer failures,' Pugie whispered to himself. 'BOO!' he shouted. 'Ha-ha-ha-ha! Your faces—you look sooo funny.'

'That was not funny. You should know better,' said Clowdie angrily.

'Wow, Clowdie—you sounded really confident; I want to try,' whispered Coco. 'Hey, you there...stinky breath,' she said.

'Oh-oh,' said Clowdie and Cuddles.

'What did you just say to me?' said Pugie.

As quick as a blink, Coco suddenly lost all of her confidence, like it had been drained out of her. Her confident smile broke into a frown, and her legs started to tremble. What had become of her? Why would she say anything as silly as that?

'**RUN!**' cried Cuddles, but Coco's legs didn't move.

'**I WANT OUR BALL BACK!**' she screamed.

Cuddles and Clowdie stopped dead in their tracks. They had forgotten all about why they had actually gone to Pugie's dump den, so they said it again slowly (a bit embarrassed) and asked for the ball.

'I don't have your silly ball. What would I want or even need it for?' Pugie said. His tail grew longer, and they saw it. He cursed his tail, wishing it wouldn't grow any longer.

'We know you have it. Your tail grew longer so that means—'

Pugie interrupted Cuddles and said, 'Yeah, so what? Even if I did have it (which I don't)...' His tail grew longer. 'Stop it, you silly tail, stop growing! I'm not giving it back to you,' Pugie said with a smirk on his face.

If there was one thing people knew about Pugie it was that he was ticklish. The pugsketeers looked at each other, and

then a big grin spread across their faces. They moved gradually closer and closer towards him, their paws out in a tickling position.

'Oh-oh,' Pugie said with a frown across his face.

Before they got any closer, he quickly told them where he had hidden the ball, so they ran off with the ball, feeling relieved.

I told you they were smart.

Chapter 4
JOURNEY TO THE PUGGING

Did I mention that Pugie pugsolutely hated his tail, especially when it grew longer because he'd lied? He never got away with it! Well, Pugie was full of strange things, but what I'm about to tell you is the strangest: Pugie wanted friends. Yes, my best beloved—Pugie wanted a friend, but for some pug-reason he did not know how to make friends. Instead, he bullied pugs and lied to them, so you can imagine how hard it was for him. Also he had been through a lot of trauma. His mother had died giving birth to him (which he blames himself for), and his father was on another land that he works on and didn't really come to visit Pugie, or really care about him. So poor Pugie was left to fend for himself. He loathed every bit about it.

Now, readers, because of this thought sprouting in his mind, he cursed and blamed his tail for not having any friends. He was so angry that he cursed a curse. I know what you're thinking: how do you curse a curse? Well, you know how angry he was; he tripped over his tail, but this time, he was so angry that he tripped and he dipped. He sobbed, and he mobbed. He cried, and he sighed. He stomped, and he jumped. He screamed, and he shrieked. He cursed, and he mursed. He shouted, and he pouted. He flopped, and he bouncy-plopped. He yammered, and he blabbered. He yelped, and he belped.

'A R G H H H H H H H H H H H H H H , ARGHHHHHHHHHHHHHHHHHHHHHH!' he screamed. Once again, my friends, he tripped on his tail. 'THAT IS THE LAST STRAW!' he cried. 'I'm going to the Pugging (Pug-King).'

Very determined, Pugie travelled all the way to Pugging Palace, and to tell you the truth, my best beloved, the whole time, Pugie's tail was trying to tell Pugie to go to the Pugging because he wanted to be short again, too.

When he got there, the tail made Pugie fall down one more time because it was going to be the last time he would trip him up (and also because he loved the good feeling he got by doing it) but what was waiting before them was going to be a big surprise as Pugie's tail, and Pugie himself, did not know that they needed patience for the tail to shrink.

When Pugie got to the Palace, he had to clean his paws before he went in even though he hated doing that, but if he wanted his tail to be short, he would have to do as he had been told.

He greeted the king in a pleasant way because that's what he had seen on Pugivision: 'Greetings, Your...um...oh, yeah, Pugajesty,' Pugie said.

The Pugging was pleased to be greeted in this special way. 'What can I do for you, child?'

Pugie told him about the curse of his tail and how his tail tripped him up now and then, and how he wanted to have friends but nobody liked him.

'I see, child. I, too, had the same problem when I was younger, and I understand how you feel.'

Pugie was amazed by this. 'Really?' he exclaimed.

'Yes, and I know a cure for this,' the Pugging said in a very confident voice. He recited the following carriwitchet: 'By the power of the Pugging, I will make your tail short and thin,' but nothing happened.

Pugie was confused.

'Ah, but that was just one part of the cure, child. You have to tell the truth to everyone for two whole days, but your tail will go back to being long if you lie within those two days.'

Chapter 5
CONFESSION TO CLOWDIE

When Pugie returned home, he did what the Pugging had said, and when he woke up on the second day, his tail was short. He couldn't believe it. He was so happy that he danced and pranced around his room. He showed it off to everyone he knew, and people came from far and wide to see it. Dogs came from the east to feast, and from the north to porth. He really wanted to fix everything he had done with all the other pugs, and he went up to them to say he was sorry, but then it was time.

It was time to say sorry to the three pugs he had hurt the most (physically and mentally): Coco, Cuddles, and Clowdie. Mostly Coco, and Clowdie, too, because Coco was shy, and Pugie bullied her for it. Clowdie because, well, he was...jealous of her. Yes, you heard me right; he was jealous of her. He actually thought she was cool, and she had the type of personality he wanted, and he **REEEEEEALLY** wanted to be friends with her, but he just didn't know how. It's a bit silly if you ask me because he bullied her, but like I said, he didn't know how to make friends.

He tried to practise in his mirror, saying the words he would say to the pugsketeers (and failed each time).

14

'Hey, guys, what's up?' he practised.

'Ugh, no—that sounded silly.

'Ooh! I know—how about this?

'Hi—um. No.

'Hey...yeah...that was it: hey, look—I am truly sorry about what I've done to you guys.

'Yeah, I can say that!' he said, finally.

Pugie (feeling very pumped) ran over to the three pugs.

Clowdie's face turned into a frown when she saw him come over. 'Oh-oh,' she said, a bit petrified.

'What is it now? Did your precious perfume run out again?' asked Cuddles in a mocking way.

'Okay, running out of perfume is a very big deal, but that's not what I'm talking about. Look!'

Cuddles rolled her eyes, but then she looked to where Clowdie was pointing, and her face dropped, and her ears stuck up. 'Q-quickly go! Take Coco with you, and I'll deal with him!'

'No! I will not allow it. I'll deal with him. Besides, I-I'm the reason he's bullying us, so **GO**!'

Pugie was out of breath and panting when he arrived because he'd sprinted all the way to the bongojo tree, and that was at least two to three metres.

Clowdie looked him up and down and rolled her eyes because she thought he was being dramatic, but she clearly hadn't run two to three metres at full speed before. She was

15

also breathing quite hard because she was really scared of what he would—or could—do.

'Sorry...just give me...a...moment,' he panted. 'Also...do you like...my tail?' he said, still bent over and panting.

Clowdie stepped back a little bit and staggered. Had Presumptuous Pugie just said SORRY? Clowdie pinched herself just to make sure she wasn't dreaming. After a few moments, she took a quick glimpse at his tail because she was curious, and she nearly fainted at that sight, too.

Pugie got up from his position, looked at Clowdie, and was very confused. 'Are you okay?'

Clowdie just stared at him, not knowing what to say. Was he talking to her or some other Clowdie he was friends with because she was pretty sure the Pugie she knew HATED her?

'Is it okay if I talk to you...please?'

Okay. Now Clowdie was really worried for him, and she turned pale. 'I'm sorry, but...do I know you?'

'Um...is that a trick question?' Pugie replied, puzzled.

'No, I'm serious—are you Pugie's twin or something? If you are, then welcome to Pugs' Premises. Just between you and me, I think you're the nicer twin.' Clowdie winked at him.

Pugie was gobsmacked. Did she really think he was someone else? Plus, he was also quite hurt that she couldn't imagine him as a kind pug, but to be honest, he hadn't really

16

been kind enough to her for her to believe he was a good pug.

'I...I...uh...um...I can't believe that you'd think that. Of course, I don't have a twin! You've known me for ages!' Pugie took a deep breath in and forced a smile.

Clowdie kind of looked creeped out by it, and she took another step back.

'Look, I'm sorry. I'm just trying to get used to this whole kind thing, but what I really came here for was to apologise because I know how mean I've been to you, and I feel really bad about it.' He paused for a moment, biting his lip, but then he carried on. 'I also want to tell you the reason why I have been this way to you, and...um...well (how do I put this?)...I guess, I was just...a bit...jealous...of how cool...you were.' Pugie looked away and turned bright red, full of embarrassment. He had never told Clowdie how he felt about her, but now that he had, he was scared of what she might think.

Clowdie's face also turned bright red. She was very flattered. She never thought Pugie had felt that way about her. Her eyes welled up with appreciative tears. She never thought anybody cared about her, especially because she knew how she acted around pugs and how rude she could get. So, because of that thought buzzing around in her head all the time, she pretended and made everybody think she was loved by everyone, so she would feel a little bit better.

Chapter 6
THE INCIDENT

After a long awkward silence, Clowdie said in a very shaky voice, 'Y-y-you r-really feel that way about...me?'

She sniffled and tried to hold her tears from pouring out.

'Y-yeah. I-I guess. It's just that...I never knew how to tell you and how to express it, and instead of me asking you if I could be your friend, I did the opposite and...well...bullied you, and I'm really sorry. Could...you please...forgive me?'

Clowdie (without thinking, as usual) hugged Pugie. And Pugie, being Pugie, freaked out. He hyperventilated and trembled all over, and then **HE FAINTED!** Since Clowdie was hugging Pugie, she fell over, too, and landed on top of him. She got up and brushed herself off, a little bit embarrassed, and she checked to see if her paws had any dirt stuck in between them.

Luckily, there wasn't any, but then she remembered that Pugie had been the reason she'd fallen over.

She went over to Pugie to see if he was all right, but

when she walked up to him, she realised that he was still on the ground. Her still flattered (but kind of embarrassed) smile turned into a frown. She thought it was a prank, and she tried to tickle him because she knew he was ticklish, but for some weird reason, he didn't wriggle around or burst out laughing—he just lay there like a dead weight.

Clowdie started to get really worried because whenever anyone tickled him, Pugie always wriggled and jiggled or laughed out loud and shouted and shouted. She trembled all over, her paws were all sweaty, and her heart seemed as if it might pound out of her chest. **WHAT DID SHE DO?** Did she kill him?

Please, don't die! Please, don't be dead! she thought. Oh, no! Oh, no!

She shook Pugie as hard as she could, feeling as nauseated as the time she'd gone to the pugspital.

Pugie didn't wake up.

She wept and ran back to Coco and Cuddles, wiping the snot and tears from her muzzle and cheeks.

Chapter 7
CLOWDIE'S PANIC ATTACK

Not looking where she was going, she bumped into her two sisters, and they all fell down.

'Hey! Watch it!' Cuddles said. 'Ugh—pugs these days! They never watch where they're going or have any respect for anyone,' she mumbled.

'Ow!' Coco said. She got up and dusted off the dirt from her fur.

Cuddles realised it was Clowdie who'd bumped into her. Hugging her, she said, 'Oh, my gosh, Clowdie—what happened with you and Pugie? Are you hurt? You have to tell us everything!' She sounded very concerned.

'Yeah, Clowdie,' said Coco We were worried about you and had to find you, so we went to look for you, and...well... you're here, but are you okay, though?'

Cuddles looked at Coco and gave her an 'I already asked Clowdie that' look, but Clowdie just glanced up at them with her wet, tear-filled eyes and sobbed and wailed.

Coco and Cuddles looked at each other, perplexed. Why was she crying? They just stood there, not knowing what to do until she stopped crying.

Coco said, in a nice and calming voice, 'What's wrong,

Clowds? You're making us worried about you. We really want to help, but we just need to know what's going on so we can do that.'

There was a long, awkward silence.

'Come on, Clowdie. We're your sissies. Please, talk to us,' Coco said again.

Clowdie finally spoke but with gasping and crying in between. 'Pugie...me...hug...fall...dead...my fault!' Clowdie cried some more.

The two girls, Coco and Cuddles, were mixed with negative and confused emotions, but they were still staggered by this news (since they kind of understood her because they were all sisters). Both of them ended up shouting at Clowdie. **'WHAT? DEAD? WHAT DO YOU MEAN, DEAD?'**

Cuddles started to get a bit aggravated at how Clowdie was just sitting there crying and not saying anything to help her understand what she'd gone through with Pugie.

'Okay, Clowdie, we know you're upset with what happened with you and Pugie, which you still need to explain later, but we are also trying to help you here! In case you didn't notice, being a cry baby will not help us at all, so, please, for Pug's sake: **TELL US WHAT HAPPENED IN A LANGUAGE WE WILL ALL UNDERSTAND! COMPRENDE?'**

Coco gave Cuddles a death stare and said, 'What is wrong with you? She is in mental distress! Can't you respect that? She

21

will tell us what happened in a moment. Just let her calm down and be patient! **COMPRENDE?**'

Chapter 8
THE REALISATION

Meanwhile, Pugie was surrounded by a lot of pugs, and they were all very confused, concerned, and startled, some of them uttering small whispers of, 'Oh, my goodness. Bless him. I bet he's poor and just sleeping,' or 'Ugh! Another one of those pests who are homeless—those little thieves!'

Cuddles and Coco were still trying to get some words out of Clowdie.

'I think I killed...Pugie...' she said finally. 'B-b-but I-I-I-I didn't...I hugged him. It's not my fault...he just fell on me. We were talking...having a good time—'

'Say what? **WHAT DID YOU JUST SAY?**' Cuddles shouted in shock.

Clowdie turned pale as chalk, and her voice quivered as she whispered, 'Th-that...w-w-we were h-having...a g-g-good t-time?'

Coco's eyes were just hollow, and she tried to take in all of the information at once as she looked quite focused on it.

'What? No. Well...yes, but that's not what I was talking about. We'll...definitely talk about that whole you and Pugie being friends thing later, but before that, you said something else.'

Clowdie's facial expression definitely showed how confused she was about what Cuddles' point was. Then she suddenly remembered what she'd said when she was rushing with her words, and she hoped her sisters hadn't heard what she'd said at the start. Her eyes sunk into her skull drowned with worry and guilt, but she finally managed the words to say, and she said it with a quiet voice: 'What I said was...I-I-I think...I killed...Pugie.' She sobbed into her paws again, feeling bad about what she thought she had done.

Coco and Cuddles' mouths hung open. Their paws shook.

Cuddles said with a whisper and a croak between her sentences, 'Y-y-you...d-d-did...what?'

Coco felt sick to her stomach. She was speechless.

Clowdie cried out loud. '**I-I-I'M...S-SORRY!**'

Coco suddenly snapped back to reality and thought about how Pugie could just be lying down dead on the floor in the middle of the ancient African desert, or how someone could kidnap his body and use it as a sacrifice to the Statue of Pugerty (in which Coco didn't believe). Plus, Coco was also pretty sure that was NOT what Pugie would have wanted.

Chapter 9
THE JOURNEY TO SAVE PUGIE

'**G**UYS! Oh, my Pugs! Guys! We have to get to Pugie... NOW,' she screamed at the top of her lungs.

'W-why?' Cuddles asked.

'Y-yeah. He's already...dead...because of...me,' Clowdie said, but her voice trailed off at the end.

'Less asking questions and more running,' Coco snapped.

Cuddles and Clowdie stood exactly where they were and looked at each other. 'We don't want to go with you,' they said in unison.

Coco sighed. 'Fine,' she said. 'You have to make a deal with me: if you sprint with me to Pugie, then I'll tell you why we have to get there.'

Cuddles and Clowdie looked at each other again, then they looked at Coco and nodded, before sprinting off.

'Okay...so what...were you...going to...say? You know... about how we...need to...hurry up...or else...something was going to happen?' said Cuddles, panting between her sentences because she was starting to run out of breath.

Coco ignored her question and dashed ahead. Having remembered the deal she'd made with them just to get them sprinting with her, she spun round and waited to let them catch up with her.

Cuddles looked at her with confusion and said, 'Why did you sprint ahead?'

'The reason why we have to be quick is because...Wait!' Coco looked around, then her straight face turned into a frown.

'**WHERE...IS...CLOWDIE?**' Coco screamed.

Cuddles shook with fear. She had never seen or heard Coco look or sound that angry before. Cuddles knew that Coco could be quite passionate about helping others (because that's what Cuddles guessed she was worrying about: helping Pugie), but she didn't know she was that passionate or that she could be that angry. Because of this, she knew something was up, and she was hiding something.

By the look Coco gave Cuddles, Cuddles knew Coco wanted her to find Clowdie.

'I'm going to find Clowdie! I'll meet you back here,' Cuddles exclaimed. Coco looked at Cuddles desperately. What a mess they'd got into.

Shortly after Cuddles had left to find Clowdie, Coco was still waiting in the dry desert. She was praying and hoping with desperation that Cuddles would come back quickly with Clowdie. She was getting really impatient and was about to storm off and go looking for her sisters, when she felt the paw of a pug tap her on the back. Startled, she turned round and pushed the pug away from her and kicking it in the knee, making her trip over too. She pulled herself up and cautiously went over to see who she had pushed, feeling a little bit guilty.

To her surprise, it was Pugie! She stepped back aghast, shaking her head in disbelief. She thought that Pugie was dead but she was wrong. She quickly bent over to help Pugie up, who was rubbing his head in pain and looking confused.

'I'm so sorry,' Coco gasped.

'I thought you were.....were....I-I don't know... You scared me. I'm sorry.'

'I-It's Ok. It's not your fault. I shouldn't have snuck up on you like that.' Pugie replied, brushing the sand and dust off his fur.

Coco was taken aback by Pugie's pleasant demeanour. What had happened to him?

'I'm really sorry Pugie. It's just that Clowdie thought you were dead and we've been running around trying to find you and now I've lost them. I don't know where they are and they could be anywhere........Oh my goodness they could be anywhere. I-I need to go!'

'Hold on,' said Pugie. 'Firstly, I'm not dead. I just fainted. Secondly, I'm really sorry to hear about your sisters. I'd like to help but....'

Coco looked at Pugie. He looked pale,

'No. You rest. I'll tell the others you're fine.'

'Coco,' can I say something?'

'Go ahead,' said Coco confused.

'I've always admired you. You're always so willing to help other people. I just wish I had brothers and sisters who looked out for me...'

His eyes welled up.

'You see, my mother died giving birth to me and my dad is working in another country. Sometimes I feel like there's no one looking out for me and I'll end up alone.'

Coco blinked. What on earth had happened to Pugie? Where was mean Pugie? She could tell he wasn't lying because his tail wasn't growing.

'You're probably wondering why I'm telling you this. I think when I fainted it did something to me...But look, there isn't time. Remember, you are a brave pug with more power than you know. Your kind heart is all the courage you need.'

Coco reached out to hug him.

'Errr, not ready for hugs just yet,' said Pugie hardening up.

Coco chuckled.

'W-wait! You might need this sack of water. I'm sorry it's all I got, but it's the best I can do since I have to head back into my den and rest. I feel drowsy and hungry. I haven't eaten all day. But when you come back with your sisters, which I know you'll do because I have faith in you, I'll come to see you."

Pugie winked at her and ran off before Coco could say

bye.

Coco smiled at him and quickly sped off with the small sack of water in her paws. She was running and running, stopped and drank some of the water because she was dying of thirst, and then started again.

Chapter 10
FINDING CLOWDIE

So Cuddles headed off, trying to look for Clowdie. 'Clowdie! Clowdie! Where are you? Oh, for Pug's sake—Clowdie, where are you? I-I know you might be traumatised by the incident with you and Pugie, but seriously, you need to come because if you don't, then you'll seriously regret it, and you will have even more guilt to pressure you. I don't know the reason why yet because Coco hasn't told me, but it sounds like something important. Plus...I think Coco's hiding something else, and I want you to help me find out what it is,' said Cuddles.

'Pleeeeease! CLOWDIE! Clowdie, look—I'm sorry, okay? I'm sorry for not being the best triplet sis to you, I really am. It's just that sometimes I get scared that you don't want to be my friend anymore because you're all grown up now, even though you're the same age as me, and that's why I tease you all the time, but sometimes you just get on my nerves. Plus, I also kept holding a grudge against you for missing my birthday to go out with Cousin Lia to the cinema. I guess that's what caused it, but now I get it. You're mature, and I accept that, but right now, you're being **REALLY ANNOYING AND IMMATURE**!' Cuddles continued. 'Oh, yeah, sorry—being mean again. I'm not really used to this nice thing, with you, especially.'

Cuddles started to get a bit frustrated with the mini search party, and she headed back to where Coco was waiting. Then, she heard a yelp that sounded like someone in pain. It was a yelp that sounded like...**CLOWDIE**.

Cuddles stopped dead in her tracks, turned as quick as a flash, and sprinted as hard as her paws would go. '**I'M COMING, CLOWDIE!**'

Cuddles' heart was beating out of her chest. Every boom of her heart rang in her ears with an echo: **BOOM! BOOM! BOOM!**

In the distance, Cuddles' eyes could just make out a round, grey shape that looked like a cave.

She ran even faster. Beads of sweat trickled down her furry cheeks and dripped off her whiskers. Her legs started to burn. Agonising pain shot up her hind legs, making them give way and causing her to fall down with a thump. Fortunately (because she ran so fast), she fell right beside the cave where (apparently) Clowdie was.

Cuddles was panting so hard that her heavy breathing made her feel faint, and the sun didn't help, either. The golden sun's gleaming rays shone down upon her back, making her fur flare up. She started to cough repeatedly. Dust sprayed everywhere.

'I'm...I'm...COUGH...COUGH...COUGH...coming...Clowdie... COUGH.' Her head spun, and she began to feel dizzy with sickness. One eye closed slowly, and then the other.

TOTAL BLACKNESS.

Chapter 11
Hiding in the Bush

Suddenly, with a jolt, Cuddles was dragged towards a bush, and drops of liquid splashed on her face. Now, my readers, I don't think I have mentioned this, but pugs, especially Cuddles, hate water, and if a tiny, single drop of water should land on their fur, they squirm and move away, even if they have passed out.

Now, back to the story.

Cuddles' fur stood on end, and her front legs tried to pull back. Then, her hind legs reeled away. Somehow, her whole body thrust back, and she pounced onto her four legs trying to attack the pug who'd tried to splash her with water. However, the pug's reflexes were way quicker than Cuddles', and she pinned Cuddles to the floor until she was calm.

Cuddles could just about turn her head to see who the pug was, and to her surprise, it was **COCO**.

'Coco!' exclaimed Cuddles.

'Shhhhhhh!' Coco got up from Cuddles and gave her a death stare.

'Why are you shushing—'

'I'm shushing you because the pugs that have Clowdie... are pugnappers, and they could hear us talking...and capture us,

33

too,' whispered Coco in a serious voice that chilled Cuddles to the bones.

After a few seconds, Cuddles had just about processed what Coco had said, and she stood there in disbelief, her eyes and mouth wide open, her body trembling all over with fear.

'H-h-how do you kn-know? W-w-we need to go and save her!' Cuddles shouted, and she sobbed into her paws, her shoulders shaking up and down.

Coco interrupted her, crying, and she said in an irritated voice, 'Oh, for Pug's sake, Cuddles—pull yourself together. And be quiet. I'm under pressure here. I couldn't wait for you any longer, so I went to find you and I'm glad I did. Pug knows what those pugnappers will do with Clowdie because we're running out of time, and the reason I know is because, when you were unconscious, I peeked inside the cave because that's obviously where you were heading, and I thought Clowdie could be there, too. I checked, and—'

'And wh-what? What happened, Coco? **TELL ME!** I'm scared,' whispered Cuddles. She looked at Coco with dull, hollow eyes.

'Well, if you'd let me talk...Ugh, I don't have time to yell at you. I saw her. She was...she was pinned to the cave wall. She looked...petrified. I wanted to pick her up and just give her a hug and...' Coco's eyes filled with tears to the brim until they gushed out, flooding her cheeks, making them damper than ever.

Cuddles saw Coco crying, and she felt bad. She tried to embrace Coco with a hug, and Coco accepted it.

Then, all of a sudden, Coco and Cuddles heard someone give another shout of pain: **CLOWDIE!**

Chapter 12
DANGER

Coco and Cuddles looked at each other with worried eyes and then looked back at the cave.

Cuddles said, 'W-was that—'

'Yes, and that means we need to hurry,' Coco said with a quiver.

Cuddles then said, 'Do you have a plan? Please, say you have a plan. I can't bear for her to be hurt.'

Coco's eyes widened. 'I-I think I have one, but I don't kn-know if it will work.'

'Well, like you said, we need to hurry,' Cuddles cried out, but then there was another voice, a lower, evil one.

'BE QUIET! No one is going to hear you because we are in the middle of the desert!' he cackled. And then there were footsteps, loud footsteps towards where Coco and Cuddles were discussing their plan.

Coco's ears pricked up when she heard the footsteps coming. She gasped. 'Get down...now. Someone's coming.'

Cuddles' reflexes told her to get down as quickly as she could to obey Coco's command, but her mouth didn't obey.

'Who's com—'

'Shushhhhhh,' whispered Coco, 'Trust me,' she replied in a reassuring voice.

36

They heard the gruff, deep voice again, but this time there were two voices, and it seemed like they were having a conversation. Because there was too much of a distance between Coco and Cuddles and the pugnappers, they couldn't quite hear everything that was said. Fortunately, Coco's ears were very alert, so she could hear most of it, but not all, especially with the gusts of wind blowing sand everywhere, which didn't really help much. Every time Coco heard the bad guys talking, the wind blew in between.

'Where's all...the...money?' the deep voice demanded.

'I...told you...already...here's...half.' The wind was too loud, and the conversation was cut off.

Coco turned to Cuddles and whispered, 'I'm too far away to hear important parts of the conversation. I need to know what's going on, what they're going to do to Clowdie. Cuddles, I-I know that you are mature enough to look after yourself here because I-I'm going to go closer towards their conversation.'

'But Coco—'

'Cuddles, look at me. Promise me you'll stay here.'

Cuddles looked at her with a glint of hope in her eyes, hoping that Coco was just joking, but then she saw that Coco was dead serious. She gave Coco the smallest fake smile she had ever made with unconvincing eyes.

Chapter 13
COCO LEAVES

Coco gave her a reassuring look, telling her that it was okay.

'Coco, you said that I was mature. If I am, then I should be able to come with you,' Cuddles whispered.

'Cuddles, you might be mature, but your mouth ain't. Plus, you know the plan. If I get caught—'

'Which you won't,' said Cuddles.

'Yeah, okay—I won't get caught. But if I do, then they'll be so distracted by me they won't realise you're trying to free Clowdie, and you'll be so far away they'll give up trying to get you. They'll just try to focus on me.'

'Yeah, but how will you get out, Coco? I can't afford to lose you, too—'

'Clowdie isn't lost. She is still with us. Plus, I know how to deal with jerks. Believe me, I know. I have an idea, and it involves outsmarting them. That is if they're dumb. Plus, you're stuck with me. You can't get rid of me yet,' Coco whispered.

She winked at Cuddles to let her know she was going to be all right, and Coco climbed carefully out of the bush, trying not to make any noise or she'd get caught.

'Coco, be careful. I also...um...love you, sis.' Cuddles tried to say this without crying her heart out, but she still had tears filled up to the brim of her eyes, making her eyesight quite blurry.

Coco also choked up, trying not to cry because she knew that if she started to cry, then Cuddles would, and they would waste time bawling on each other's shoulders hugging.
'Oh, come here, you big baby,' Coco teased Cuddles.

Cuddles threw herself onto Coco, and they stood there hugging for a few seconds, but then Coco pulled herself away and said she had to go, and also, that Cuddles should remember the signal. She quickly ran to the other big-hedge-kind-of-looking-bush and hid there, trying to listen to the conversation.

Chapter 14
THE DELETERIOUS CONVERSATION

'This pug girl is very expensive and her kind of breed is very rare, so it's either you give me the full amount of pay, or you don't get the pug,' the deep voice said.

'He must mean Clowdie. Ugh...those boneheads are messing with the wrong pugs. No one is selling my sister on my watch,' Coco whispered to herself.

Coco heard another voice she recognised. It was the one that the wind cut off when she was trying to listen to the conversation with Cuddles. 'Look, if you don't believe that I'm going to give you the rest of the money, then I'll leave something here, so that when I come back with the money, I'll have it back. Do we have a deal?'

Coco tried separating the leaves to see the two bad dogs. When she saw them, she was gobsmacked; she was paralysed to her spot. They were huge and bulky. One had a huge scar, running down from the eye to the chin, and the other had an eye missing. It looked like one of those deep, menacing, black holes in space. It was so hollow and empty, that even his emotions and soul could get lost in it. The pug with the low voice (Coco presumed was The Scar Pug) hardly looked convinced at all.

'What if you come at night-time and take the thing you leave here?' The Scar Pug said.

'Are you seriously kidding me right now?' shouted The Lost-Eye Pug. 'Why don't you trust me? I would never do that... you know I won't do that! Plus I won't risk making you think I'm dishonest....I know I've already lost some of your trust with your money....but I'm trying to gain back your trust. Also, you have some pretty great deals, and if you want to keep getting big wads of cash coming in, then you shouldn't be so uptight. Relax.'

The Scar Pug grumbled. He didn't seem quite happy with what The Lost-Eye Pug had said. His eyes narrowed into a frown. 'Who are you to tell me to not be uptight? Aren't you the person who made me 'stingy', Oscar? Aren't you? It's hard to trust anyone after what you did to me—I apologised and—apologies aren't enough! Do you know what I went through?'

The Scar Pug sighed and then looked at The Lost-Eye Pug 'Fine...You know what...I-I'm going to give you a chance. If you ruin it, then you'll wish you never came here, or met me.'

The Lost-Eye Pug gave The Scar Pug a big wad of cash and then took off his pendant and gave it to The Scar Pug. They both shook paws and made their way to the cave.

Chapter 15
COCO'S MISTAKE

As soon as they started walking away, Coco stumbled and tripped over a twig. 'Oh, fudgecake!' she muttered under her breath.

The two bad pugs were just about to step inside the cave, but once they heard Coco snap the twig, they stopped dead in their tracks, changed the direction they were heading in, and moved towards the hedge-like-looking-bush.

'Did you hear something?' The Scar Pug said as they moved towards it.

The Lost-Eye Pug looked at The Scar Pug, and then he looked at the bush. He nodded.

Coco's heart was hammering out of her skin. The silence was deafening with anticipation. Should she try to escape? No, she couldn't. Clowdie would be all alone. Her blood rushed to her ears, making her feel sick to her stomach. Coco was paralysed in her spot once again.

'Hello? I know you're hiding here somewhere. You'd better come out now because if we find you, you'll wish you never set foot in this place!' said The Scar Pug.

'H-help!'

Oh, no. That must be Clowdie, Coco thought. She sounds

like she's in pain. Oh, Clowdie, I'll get you out soon. I'll sort out these knuckleheads, just you wait.

'Be quiet you **TWANG**,' The Scar Pug shouted.

Coco gasped in shock. He had the audacity to speak to her sister like that with such utter disrespect! Not on her watch, he didn't!

'Wait!' The Lost-Eye Pug said, 'Did you hear that?'

The Scar Pug looked at him in a confused way. 'Hear what?'

'A rustling sound. It sounds like it's coming from the bushes. Over there,' The Lost-Eye Pug said. Then he whispered, 'I have an idea.'

The Scar Pug gave him a 'go on then' look, and The Lost-Eye carried on: 'If we pretend to walk off then the pug might come out, thinking that we've gone. As soon as he or she comes out, we pounce right into action and take the pug away.'

The Scar Pug didn't look convinced. 'And if it doesn't work?' he whispered.

The Lost-Eye Pug rolled his eye. 'You never think the best of me or my ideas,' he hissed.

'Fine, then. If you want things to be complicated, instead of just following my plan A, we'll go to plan B: we sneak up on the pug, and we grab the pug and take it away. You happy now, party pooper?' The Scar Pug mimicked The Lost-Eye Pug under his breath, looked at him, and nodded with an irritated sigh.

43

They tiptoed towards the bush, and quick as a flash, grabbed Coco by the neck.

Coco's heart leapt out of her skin. Blood oozed from her paw as a piece of flesh had been caught by a thorn in the bush.

Chapter 16
CAPTURED

'Well, well, well...look who we have here!'

Coco thrust about in The Scar Pug's grip. Whenever she kicked or moved, he tightened his grip.

'Well, I have to give it to ya. Your plan was pretty impressive and successful, coz if it wasn't for you, then I wouldn't have had a double package.' He looked down at Coco and smirked.

'**GET OFF ME, YOU TWANG!**' Coco shouted.

The Scar Pug looked flabbergasted, probably because he didn't expect a little girl pug to swear, but then his confused expression turned to a frown as he was offended. The Lost-Eye Pug, on the other hand, looked like he was holding in a laugh because he found it really funny. He almost looked a bit proud that someone had taught The Scar Pug a lesson and cursed at him.

'Yeah, that's right—see how you like it. You called my sister a twang, so I have every right to call you one. Plus, you deserve it, and you are one, even if you hadn't called my sister one.' Coco spat on his arm whilst saying that.

'**WHO THE DING-DONG-HEAD IS YOUR SISTER?**' The Scar Pug hissed through gritted teeth.

'MY SISTER IS THE ONE YOU ARE PRESENTLY HOLDING CAPTIVE!'

The corners of The Scar Pug's mouth lifted up from a frown into a smug-looking smile, rising up like a helium balloon reaching for the blue blanket up above. 'Oh...ha...you mean that nutjob in the cave over there? Well, I never. I guess the craziness runs in the family,' The Scar Pug said.

Coco reached down to bite him. She locked her jaw filled with fangs and bit through his fur and into his flesh.

The Scar Pug's face turned chalk white. His grip on her released, and he bellowed out an agonising, ear-piercing shriek: '**AHHHHHHHHHHHH! GET OFF ME, YOU LITTLE PIECE OF—**'

'As you command,' she mumbled. She let go, but instead of letting go with her mouth unlocked, she came down and yanked out a big chunk of fur.

He let out another scream.

She spat the fur from her mouth and sprinted as far as her little four legs could carry her, leading them to a place where they would be taken good care of. '**CAW...CAW! CAW... CAW!**' she screamed at the top of her lungs.

Chapter 17
THE RESCUE MISSION

Meanwhile, Cuddles was still hiding behind a bush. '1,999 Mississippi...2000 Mississippi...

'Oh, my Pug! It's the signal! Okay, Cuddles—you know what to do.

'Ummm...oh, yeah. Oh, my Pug...oh, my Pug...oh, my Pug!

'Okay...breathe, Cuddles. You can do this...your sisters need you, and it's up to you to save them.

'THREE...TWO...ONE...RUUUUUUUUN!'

Cuddles ran and ran and ran and ran. 'The cave! Oh, my pug the cave,' she muttered to herself, out of breath.

She caught her breath and tried to peer inside. 'Jeez, this place gives me bad vibes and the heebie-jeebies.'

Cuddles gasped. **CLOWDIE!**

'No...Clowdie! Oh, my Pug!' Cuddles sprinted over to Clowdie and flopped beside her, not thinking twice about getting caught.

Clowdie's eyes looked like they had sunken into her skull, and they were closed shut. Beads of sweat rippled down her cheeks, evaporating as they hit the floor. Her body trembled all over. Her head was probably filled with traumatic fear. She whispered, 'Help! Help! Please!' She shook her head.

Cuddles got scared and worried. 'Clowdie, I'm here!' she said. 'Clowdie, please stop—you're scaring me! Wake up, Clowdie! Wake up! It's probably just a nightmare! You're fine because I'm here now.'

Cuddles hugged her to try to calm her down, stroking Clowdie's fur, but Clowdie winced.

Cuddles pulled away from her to see what was wrong. She saw that her arm was bruised, really bruised, and her hind leg had a deep cut. It looked like it might have been made by a whip. Cuddles roared with rage. 'Who would do this to you?'

Clowdie's eyes suddenly snapped open. Her eyes looked dull, like all the colour from her pupils had drained out of them.

'Oh, my Pug! Clowdie, you're awake!'

'Cuddles,' was all Clowdie managed to croak.

'Yes! Yes! I'm here! I'm here.' Cuddles started to cry, and so did Clowdie but very softly.

Chapter 18
THE ESCAPE

'We need to get you out of here...like now!'

Clowdie just stared. She didn't move a muscle.

Well, she probably couldn't because her muscles would have hurt.

Cuddles looked at Clowdie, but then she realised that Clowdie's other hind leg was pinned to a fabric nailed to the wall of the cave. Cuddles gasped in horror. 'They...they did that to you? These dogs mean business. Okay...okay, Clowdie, can you walk?'

'I...I don't know,' Clowdie croaked.

'Okay, well, after I bust you out of here, I'm still trying to figure out what to do. We **NEED** to run...or in your case, power walk.'

'Coco, wh-where's Coco?'

'Oh...um...She's fine...I hope. She promised she'll be fine.' In the corner of her eye, Cuddles caught a glimpse of something glistening in the reflection of the dappled sun. 'Wait a minute—what...what's that?' Cuddles ran over to the thing she'd seen in the corner of her eye and picked it up. She grinned so wide until her lips ached. 'It's a dagger, Clowdie. It's a dagger, eee!'

Cuddles ran back to Clowdie, and without thinking

49

whether or not Clowdie wanted it to happen, she sawed at the fabric.

One nail fell off. Then another. Then **ANOTHER** until the last one fell off.

'Yay Clowdie—you're free!' Cuddles hugged Clowdie once more, but this time, more cautiously.

Clowdie staggered up to her paws with shaky legs. She tried to walk, but her legs gave way, and she fell.

'Oh, Clowdie. Um...okay...maybe you can...get on my back?' Clowdie hobbled over to Cuddles, falling twice.

'Come on—three, two, one...there we go.' Cuddles started walking and then faster, into a power walk, then into a run, and finally, into a sprint.

'Wow...you're...actually...quite light,' she managed to get out with a pant. She ran and ran, but then she started to slow down because she recognised the place.

'IT'S OUR BONGOJO TREE, CLOWDIE! THE TREE THE PARENTS DANCE AROUND! We're here, Clowdie!'

Chapter 19
THE REUNION

'W'e're home!'

'Yeah, we are!' screamed Coco, on purpose, to scare them.

'Arghh!' shouted Cuddles.

Clowdie and Cuddles turned around.

'Coco!'

'Coco!'

They embraced in a three-way hug.

'Oh, my Pug, Clowdie. I'm so happy you're all right. And Cuddles...I'm proud of you. You got home with Clowdie like I asked. No offence or anything, but I'm surprised this whole thing was a success, especially with you in it, Cuddles.'

Cuddles pretended to put on an offended face, but then she burst out laughing and couldn't stop. When she calmed down, she said, 'To be honest, I probably wouldn't have trusted myself either, but anyway, enough about Coco and me. We need to get you to the medical centre, Clowdie. What happened with you and those thugs, Coco?'

'Well, let's just say they're in good hands with a bear in another cave,' Coco replied.

'Well, they do deserve it,' Cuddles said with a smirk.

Clowdie nodded and smiled.

Coco's ears pricked up once more.

'What's wrong?' asked Clowdie.

Coco didn't answer. All she did was smile. 'He's fine,' Coco said at last.

'Who's fine? What's going on?' Cuddles said.

'Pugie. Pugie's fine. He's coming this way. Look!' exclaimed Coco, excitedly.

Clowdie's face turned pale. 'What?' Her head swivelled round in the direction Coco was pointing, and her mouth dropped. He really was alive.

'Hi,' Pugie said with a smile.

Cuddles just stared, and so did Clowdie, but Coco smiled.

'Ohhh—did you think I was dead?' he said as if he'd read their minds. 'No, I just fainted because Clowdie hugged me, and I haven't been hugged in a long time, so it was a shock to me.'

Clowdie blushed. She felt so silly. She'd thought he was dead, and she'd made such a big scene out of it when really, he'd just fainted.

'And also,' Pugie carried on, 'Coco wanted me to tell you that I was helping her to be more confident, and I hope that's been a success.'

Since he was getting the hang of telling the truth (like the Pugging had asked), he was starting to share a little too much information in the effort of being more truthful. I don't think Coco was ready for Pugie to say anything about her secretly meeting up with him to be taught how to be more confident.

Chapter 20
A NEW FRIEND

'Whaaaaat? I-I knew something was different about your personality, but Coco, you didn't have to do that behind our backs or even change your whole personality. We loved the way you were. And also, was that the thing you were hiding from us?' Cuddles asked.

Pugie gave a look in Coco's direction, and so did the other pugs. Now it was her turn to blush. She sighed. 'Yes,' she replied to Cuddles' question, but then she continued with what she was going to say. 'And i-it wasn't for you that I changed; it was for me. I was sick of being shy and being bullied.' She paused for a second but then carried on talking: 'So, I thought I should go to someone to help me be confident, and I thought Pugie because he's the most confident pug I know. Of course, it wasn't easy, but he really helped, and the answer to your question is...yes, it was successful.' She did a really big grin and everyone else smiled with her.

'Sorry to break the moment of happiness here, but I also wanted to tell you that I have a new tail because I don't lie anymore.' Pugie also grinned and turned around to show off his tail as he wiggled it around.

Everyone was stunned apart from Coco because she had

already seen it.

'And lastly, I came to ask if we...um...could we...all be friends maybe? I mean, you don't have to if you don't want to.' Coco looked round at her sisters, and they all slowly nodded.

From then on, they were no longer the three pugsketeers; they were the four pugsketeers. Coco was known for her courage, Clowdie was known for her fashion, Cuddles was known for her rescuing, and Pugie was known for his tail that had grown short because he told the truth. No longer was Pugie presumptuous—he was playful and kind, and his dream to have friends had come true.

And that is the story of how the pug got its short tail.

THE END...OR IS IT JUST THE BEGINNING?

Acknowledgments

Special thank you to God for the inspiration and to my mum and dad for inspiring and encouraging me to write and publish this book.

Thank you to all my sponsors listed below for encouraging and supporting me with publishing my debut book:

Grandpa Safaru Adewale Mustapha, Grandma Victoria Oyegunle, Uncle Seun and Tosin Mustapha, Uncle John Oyegunle, Grandpa Daddy Oyegunle, Aunty Janet Oye, Grandma Adetutu, Uncle Gideon John, Aunty Nosa, Uncle Jonathan John, Grandma and Grandpa Oluwole-Rotimi, Auntie Yeni Fakorede, Auntie Tola Okogwu, Aunty Eloho Efemua, Aunty Lánre Njoku, Carlie Sorosiak, Allison Buchanan, Fayefaye Thompson, Pastor Temilolu Odejide, Debo Oshungboye, Olayemi Oluwadimu, Abi Olabode, Ellen Pickard, Jummy Oladiran, Aunty Sumbo Aseru, Enny Owolabi, Bharti Dhir, Abigail Morakinyo, Amie Newby, Marian ewetade, Vivien Palmer, Morounfolu Olatuja, Natalie Joseph, Uncle Tunde Babs, Holly Coleman, Anthony Onifade, Autism From the Outside, Folake Adegbola, Abimbola Akonmade, Lara Ajai, Temi Esho, Aunty Subrina McCalla, Gerald, H Richards, Shireen Quadir, Rita Okeke, Claudia Telcar Evans, Aunty Bolanle Johnson, Aunty Jums, Grandma Anthonia Owolabi, Yejide Fadipe Aunty Esther Olaleye, Ade, Albert, Laitan, Dee Bailey, Grace Amure, Uncle Segun and Aderinsola Laniyan, Elizabeth Opaleye, Aunty Nkem Ogidi, Adebola Osiyemi, Ugochi Anyanwu, Azeez, Ranti O, Gelila, Opeyemi Abebe, Uba Anaiya Ariella Barbara, Layi Shonubi, Funmi S and Uncle Shola Akinsanmi.

Can't forget my friends Lucia and Ollie who listened to me and shared ideas with me during the writing process.

About the Author

My name is Joanah Adewale, but my friends call me Jojo and I am currently 12 years old. I have one sister who everyone loves and my loving parents. I love drama with a passion and I'm a dancer. I also want to be an actress, but I definitely enjoy writing stories. One of my favourite places to go is a theme park because I love rollercoasters and the thrill gets me all excited.

Conscious Dreams
P U B L I S H I N G

Transforming diverse writers
into successful published authors

 www.consciousdreamspublishing.com

 authors@consciousdreamspublishing.com

Let's connect

CPSIA information can be obtained
at www.ICGtesting.com
Printed in the USA
LVHW050622110622
720906LV00004B/6